A Furry Fiasco

Read more Animal Inn books!

BOOK 2: Treasure Hunt

Coming soon:

BOOK 3: The Bow-wow Bus

ANIMAL INN
A Furry Fiasco

Book 1

PAUL DUBOIS JACOBS
&
JENNIFER SWENDER

Illustrated by STEPHANIE LABERIS

ALADDIN
New York   London   Toronto   Sydney   New Delhi

ALADDIN

An imprint of Simon & Schuster Children's Publishing Division

1230 Avenue of the Americas, New York, New York 10020

First Aladdin paperback edition December 2016

Text copyright © 2016 by Simon & Schuster, Inc.

Illustrations copyright © 2016 by Stephanie Laberis

Also available in an Aladdin hardcover edition.

All rights reserved, including the right of reproduction in whole or in part in any form.

ALADDIN and related logo are registered trademarks of Simon & Schuster, Inc.

For information about special discounts for bulk purchases, please contact

Simon & Schuster Special Sales at 1-866-506-1949 or business@simonandschuster.com.

The Simon & Schuster Speakers Bureau can bring authors to your live event. For more information or to book an event, contact the Simon & Schuster Speakers Bureau at 1-866-248-3049 or visit our website at www.simonspeakers.com.

Cover designed by Jessica Handelman

Interior designed by Greg Stadnyk

The illustrations for this book were rendered digitally.

The text of this book was set in Bembo Std.

Manufactured in the United States of America 1116 OFF

2 4 6 8 10 9 7 5 3 1

Library of Congress Control Number 2016936112

ISBN 978-1-4814-6224-2 (hc)

ISBN 978-1-4814-6223-5 (pbk)

ISBN 978-1-4814-6225-9 (eBook)

For Jennifer Weltz

PROLOGUE

Ding-dong!

Ding-dong!

Our doorbell is always ringing.

Ding-dong!

Welcome to Animal Inn. My name is Leopold
Augustus Gonzalo Tyler. I am a scarlet macaw.

No, I am not the loopy bird you see on that
breakfast cereal box. That is a toucan. I am a

macaw. Macaws are intelligent and dignified creatures. Toucans are clumsy and make a racket.

Our family began with Mom, Dad, me, and our Tibetan terrier, Dash. I suppose I should also mention their human sons, Jake and Ethan.

Five years ago Cassie was born. She's a human girl.

Four years ago we adopted Coco, a chocolate Labrador retriever.

Three years ago Shadow and Whiskers showed up at our door. They are sister and brother cats.

And one year ago Jake and Ethan won Fuzzy and Furry at the school fair. They are a pair of very adventurous gerbils.

We used to live in an apartment in the city. But when kid number three and dog number two joined the family, Mom and Dad bought this old house in the country.

Animal Inn is one part hotel, one part school, and one part spa. As our brochure says, *We promise to love your pet as much as you do.*

Ding-dong!

Would someone please answer the door?

It could be a Pekinese here for a pedicure. A Siamese for a short stay. Or a llama for a long stay. We've even had an otter sign up for swim lessons. It's no wonder the doorbell is always ringing.

On the first floor of Animal Inn, we have the Welcome Area, the office, the classroom, the party and play room, and the grooming room.

Our family, the Tyler family, lives on the second floor. This includes Fuzzy and Furry locked in their gerbiltorium in Jake and Ethan's room. (More about this later.)

The third floor is for smaller animals. Any guest

who needs an aquarium, a terrarium, or a solarium stays on the third floor.

Ding-dong!

Where is everybody?

Maybe they're out in the barn and kennels. That's where the larger animals stay.

Here at Animal Inn we can provide just about any habitat a guest might need. Hot, cold, wet, dry, forest, desert. We've got it all.

"Habitat" is just a fancy word for "home." We recently added a new habitat. The first guest to stay there caused quite a stir.

Let me tell you what happened a few weeks ago. . . .

CHAPTER
1

It began like any other Saturday

morning.

Saturday is a busy day at Animal Inn. Mom teaches her Polite Puppies class. Dad and Jake host the Furry Pages. That's when children read aloud to an animal buddy. And there are grooming appointments and usually a birthday party or two.

On this Saturday morning I was on my perch

in the Welcome Area. Dad was tidying up the brochures. Mom was talking on the phone to an old friend from her dog show days.

Suddenly I heard Jake holler from upstairs. "Where could they be?"

"I don't know," shouted Ethan. "They were in the gerbiltorium a minute ago."

Fiddlesticks. Fuzzy and Furry must have escaped again.

Fuzzy and Furry are experts at picking the lock on their gerbiltorium. They usually escape at night, when guests are safely tucked into their cages, crates, tanks, and stalls.

I was a bit worried that Fuzzy and Furry might run into the new guest on the third floor—a boa constrictor named Copernicus.

"Ethan!" Jake shouted. "Start looking!"

"Stop telling me what to do!" Ethan shouted.

"Ethan! Start looking!" Jake shouted again.

"You're not the boss of me!" Ethan shouted back.

Mom rushed up the stairs. Luckily, the gerbils had not bumped into Copernicus. They were found in Jake and Ethan's laundry hamper, fast asleep.

A few minutes later Cassie came downstairs, followed by Coco.

"Princess Coco," Cassie said, "let's go look for fairies."

"Just have Coco back in time for Furry Pages," said Dad. "And careful not to let Shadow out."

Shadow is supposed to be an indoor cat, but she loves to sneak outside. Cassie and Coco are her best chance for a little adventure.

"Dad," Cassie said. "We are princesses. I am *Princess* Cassie, and this is *Princess* Coco."

"My apologies," Dad said, and smiled. He bowed to them. "I'll be in the basement if you need me."

"I can't believe it!" Cassie whispered to Coco as soon as Dad left. "I just can't believe it!"

I perked up my ears. Yes, I do have ears. They're hidden under my feathers.

What was it that Cassie found so unbelievable?

Like many other five-year-old humans, she can get very excited. "I can't believe it!" is one of her favorite things to say.

Pizza for dinner? I can't believe it!

That hermit crab's name is Banjo? I can't believe it!

Coco gave a tremendous shake. Luckily, one of Jake's Saturday chores is sweeping up the Welcome Area. And after any shake by Coco, the Welcome Area can use a good sweep.

"I can't believe it," Cassie said again, and giggled.

She headed back upstairs. Coco started to follow.

"Ahem." I cleared my throat.

Coco got the message. She stopped in front of my perch.

"*What* is going on?" I whispered.

"So . . . ," Coco started, "Mom was on the phone. Then the gerbils got lost. Then Ethan got mad at Jake for being bossy. Then the gerbils got found. Then Cassie and I were princesses. Then we—"

"Not *that*," I interrupted. "What is it that Cassie can't believe?"

"Oh," said Coco. "Cassie can't believe a lot of things. She can't believe it's almost September. She can't believe it might rain today. She can't believe there's mac-and-cheese for lunch. I love mac-and-cheese. Do you like mac-and-cheese, Leopold?"

I knew it had been a mistake to start a conversation

with Coco. "No," I said. "Macaws do not like mac-and-cheese."

"Really?" Coco gasped. "Mac-and-cheese is my favorite. I always hang out under the table on mac-and-cheese day. Cassie has trouble fitting all those little noodles onto her fork. Some fall onto the floor. Yummy!" Coco licked her lips.

This conversation was getting me nowhere. "Never mind," I said.

Coco started for the stairs. "By the way," she said over her shoulder, "did you hear about the wizard who's coming? Cassie can't believe *that* either."

CHAPTER
2

It wasn't long before Whiskers

scurried down the stairs.

"This is *Animal* Inn," he said worriedly. "A wizard is not an animal."

Hmm. Here was another pet talking about a wizard. "What are you fretting about?" I asked.

"Haven't you heard? A new guest is coming." Whiskers gulped. "It's a wizard!"

"Did you say 'wizard'?" Shadow asked, popping out from behind the sofa. "That's so cool!"

"I don't think it's cool," said Whiskers. "What if the wizard casts a spell on us? What if it turns us into houseflies or . . . slugs?"

"That would be awesome!" said Shadow.

"No, it wouldn't," Whiskers replied, trembling.

"Little Brother," said Shadow, "don't be such a scaredy-cat."

Ding-dong!

"The wizard is here!" Whiskers screeched. He jumped straight into the air with his fur raised on end.

Shadow snuck back bchind the sofa.

Mom and Cassie came downstairs to answer the door. I raised one wing to tell Mom that, yes, Shadow was hiding behind the sofa.

"Thank you, Leopold," she said.

"Thank you, Leopold," I repeated.

Mom smiled. It makes Mom smile when she thanks me and then I thank myself. And I love to see Mom smile. She opened the door.

To my surprise it really was . . .

Not a wizard. It was a puppy.

The puppy was having a birthday party after Polite Puppies class. His family had arrived early to decorate the room with balloons and streamers.

Mom let them in and quickly closed the door. Then she and Cassie led the birthday pup and his family to the party room.

"Good morning, Shadow," Mom called as she passed by the sofa.

"Okay, wise guys," Shadow huffed at us. "Who told her I was hiding here?"

"Let's focus," I said. "When is this wizard supposed

to arrive?"

"Soon," said a voice from the stairs. It was Dash.

It's one thing to hear something from goofy

Coco or nervous Whiskers. But when Dash says

something, it's usually true. He and I have been

 15

with the Tylers the longest. He's been their pet even longer than I have.

"This is terrible," Whiskers whimpered.

"We'll be fine," said Dash calmly. "We just need a plan."

"I've got it," said Whiskers. "I'll distract the wizard with a yowl. Leopold, you snatch his wand and fly it to Dash. Dash, you run and bury the wand in the backyard. No more magic."

"But what if the wizard doesn't use a wand?" Shadow asked. "What if he uses only magic words, such as 'hocus-pocus'?"

"Or 'presto,'" said Dash.

"Or 'abracadabra,'" I added.

Just then Jake and Ethan came downstairs.

Dash sat.

Shadow hid.

Whiskers pretended to sleep on the sofa.

And I squawked, "Abracadabra! Abracadabra!"

"That's a new one, Leopold," said Ethan. He went to join Mom and Cassie for Polite Puppies.

"Come on, Dash. Come on, Leopold," said Jake. "It's time for us to get ready for Furry Pages."

"Listen," Dash whispered to me on the way to the classroom. "I'm telling only *you* this. I don't want to get the others all worked up."

"What is it?" I asked.

"I overheard the boys talking. The wizard is not the guest," Dash said. "The wizard is the owner."

"The owner of what?" I asked. "An owl? A bat?"

"No," whispered Dash. "A dragon."

CHAPTER
3

"Maybe they were talking about
a *make-believe* dragon," I said.

"I don't think so," whispered Dash. "I heard Dad
say we need an extra fire extinguisher. And you
know what kind of animal breathes fire."

"Fiddlesticks," I said. "This isn't good."

As the children arrived, they arranged their
carpet squares on the floor. Jake passed out books

to the children who were already sitting.

"We really need a plan," said Dash. "First step, we need information."

"Good morning, everyone," Jake announced. "Welcome to Furry Pages."

Dad hurried into the classroom. "Sorry I'm late," he said.

"We'll have to talk more later," Dash whispered. He headed to an empty carpet square.

Today's books were from the Henry and Mudge series. Henry is a small boy. Mudge is his big dog.

Everybody wanted to sit with Dash. He let himself be patted and pet as the children read. You would never know that he had dangerous dragons and wizards on his mind. Maybe the stories were helping him forget.

I made my best attempt to bark like a dog. A young boy with a runny nose and a determined look came over. He had a copy of *Henry and Mudge and the Happy Cat*.

The story is about a stray cat that shows up at Henry and Mudge's door. The book took me back to the day when Shadow and Whiskers showed up on our doorstep.

"And speaking of big, lovable dogs," Jake announced. "Here's Coco."

Coco lumbered into the room.

"Better late than never," I squawked out loud. Everybody laughed.

Coco is *never* on time. And she can never sit still. Furry Pages is a challenge for her. She usually comes late, leaves early, and naps in between.

Coco flopped down onto an empty carpet square. A couple of the kids who had been reading with Dash moved over to her. Within a few minutes I could hear her softly snoring. Well, I guess that *is* the sign of a good bedtime story.

While the kids read, the parents chatted quietly. Jake passed out people snacks and dog snacks, too.

He helped children sound out difficult words.

I couldn't understand how Jake could be so calm. Wasn't he nervous about the new guest?

"Was that the doorbell?" Dad asked. *He* seemed nervous.

"I didn't hear anything," said Jake.

Dad pulled a crumpled to-do list from his back pocket. He checked it. He checked his watch. He checked the clock on the wall. He checked his list again. He checked—

Ding-dong!

Dad jumped.

"That's *definitely* the doorbell," he said. "Jake, you're in charge. It must be the supplies for you-know-who!"

I looked at Dash. Dash looked at me.

"I hope I didn't forget anything," said Dad,

checking his list again. "Fire Chief Morales will be here this afternoon to inspect the basement."

Basement? What was happening in the basement?

"Relax, Dad," Jake said, and smiled.

Relax? I thought. Was this really a time to relax?

"We need to be extra safe," said Dad. "We need to make sure everything meets fire code."

"I know," said Jake. "But what are the chances that our new guest is *actually* going to breathe fire?"

A guest that breathes fire?

Gulp.

CHAPTER
4

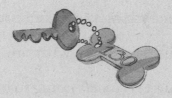

After Furry Pages, I flew back
to the Welcome Area. My mind was fluttering
faster than my wings. I could barely hear myself
think.

Yip! Yip! Yap! Yap! Yap!

Puppies, puppies, and even more puppies were
arriving for the birthday party.

Yap! Yap!

Mom, Ethan, and Cassie were doing their best to guide the guests into the party room.

I settled on my perch. When I looked down, one of the puppies was gnawing on my wooden post.

"Young fellow," I said, "would you please stop?"

The gnawing continued. I let out a loud squawk. That did the trick. The puppy ran off to join the others.

Whiskers jumped down from his spot on the sofa. "What are we going to do, Leopold?" he asked nervously.

"Dash and I are working on a plan," I assured him.

Whiskers buried his head in his paws. "Let's just hide," he said.

"Why hide?" said Shadow, popping out from

behind the sofa. "This place could use some real excitement."

At the moment it seemed plenty exciting to me. A puppy party is a noisy party. I looked over to the party room. Mom was fixing some streamers that had fallen down. Ethan was organizing a game.

When Cassie wasn't hugging the party guests, they were tearing around the room. They sniffed and investigated everything—the treats table, the presents table, the box of supplies for Pin the Tail on the Kitty. They looked like a pack of very small, four-legged detectives.

Detectives! That was what we needed.

Dash came into the Welcome Area from Furry Pages after the last child had left.

"I know who can help us gather information," I said excitedly. "Follow me to the gerbiltorium!"

Dash and I raced up the stairs. We went straight to Jake and Ethan's room. The coast was clear.

"Hi, Dash," said Fuzzy.

"Hi, Leopold," added Furry. "What's up?"

"We've got a job for you," I said. "But it could be dangerous."

"'Danger' is our middle name," said Fuzzy. He was crunching on a piece of celery.

"What's in it for us?" added Furry.

"Two dog biscuits," said Dash.

"They need to be whole," said Fuzzy.

"No crumbs," added Furry.

"Deal," said Dash.

"You won't be disappointed," said Fuzzy.

"We're the best in the business," added Furry.

"But you don't even know what the job is yet," I said.

"Doesn't matter," said Fuzzy. "'Danger' is our first name."

"I thought 'Danger' was your middle name," Dash said.

"Well, actually, 'Danger' is our last name," said Furry.

"It is?" said Fuzzy. "I thought our last name was 'Tyler.'"

"Guys," said Dash, "let's focus. We need you to sneak down to the basement. Then report back to us. Tell us everything you see and hear."

"We're depending on you," I said. "This can't fail."

"'Can't fail' is our middle name," said Fuzzy.

"We have lots of middle names," added Furry.

"My full name," Fuzzy said, "is actually Fuzzy Danger Can't Fail Tyler."

"See, Leopold. You're not the only one with a long, fancy name," added Furry.

They both giggled and began to pick the lock on the gerbiltorium.

CHAPTER
5

Dash and I made our way downstairs.

Whiskers was back on the sofa. He looked even more worried than before.

The front door was wide open, and there was a truck in the driveway. Dad was helping a delivery person unload boxes onto a dolly. There was a light rain, so the boxes were covered with a tarp.

"That's strange," said Dash. "We don't usually get deliveries on Saturday."

"What do you think it is?" I asked.

Shadow slunk out from behind the sofa. "Only one way to find out," she said. She started for the open door.

"Don't go near that truck, Shadow," Whiskers begged. "Remember what happened last time?"

"True," said Dash, "but more information could be helpful."

"I'll be fine, Whiskers," Shadow said. And she slipped out the door.

"Everything is going downstairs," Dad said, wiping off his wet boots. He crossed the Welcome Area and opened the basement door for the delivery person.

I flew over to my perch. Out the window I could

see Shadow sitting in the driver's seat of the delivery truck.

"Can you see her, Leopold?" Whiskers asked.

I nodded. "Same as last time. Paws on the steering wheel."

"Let's hope the keys aren't in the ignition this time," Dash said.

Dash came over and placed his two front paws on the windowsill. We both watched as Shadow scampered from the driver's seat into the back of the truck.

"Best party ever!"

It was Coco, stumbling in from the party room. She had cake frosting all over her snout. "Hey, what are you guys looking at?" She came over next to Dash.

"It's Shadow." I pointed with one wing. "She's in that truck."

"Ooh," said Coco. "She's going to get in trouble."

Dad and the delivery person came up from the basement. Dash quickly took his paws off the windowsill.

"Well, nothing's getting out of there," said the delivery person, pointing downstairs.

"Hope not," said Dad.

"Good luck," said the delivery person. He left and shut the front door.

"Plus," Dad said to himself, "it's too late to turn back now."

Too late to turn back? I thought.

I looked at Dash. He looked as worried as I felt.

Dad headed back down to the basement.

Dash put his paws back up onto the windowsill to check on Shadow. But before he could spot her, a dozen puppies bounded out of the party room.

Yip! Yip! Yap! Yap! Yap!

The party was officially over. Jake, Ethan, and Cassie were making sure every guest had a goody bag.

Yap! Yap!

Mom opened the front door. As the gaggle of puppies bounced out, Shadow snuck back in.

"How about some lunch?" Mom asked the kids.

"Sounds great," said Ethan. "I'm so hungry, I could eat a puppy treat."

The Tylers headed upstairs.

"Shadow! What a relief. You're safe." Whiskers sighed.

"For now," said Shadow. She looked more than a little worried.

"What do you mean?" Whiskers asked.

Shadow looked around nervously. "There were

lots of boxes in that truck." She shivered.

I held my breath.

"Some of the boxes were labeled *Exotic Animal Supplies.*"

"What does 'exotic' mean?" asked Coco.

"It means 'unusual,'" I said.

"Or 'from a different land,'" added Dash.

"Well, that doesn't sound too bad," said Coco.

"It's not," said Shadow. "But some of the boxes were labeled *Dangerous-Animal Containment System.*"

"Did you say . . . 'dangerous'?" Whiskers trembled.

"I don't get it," said Coco. "Why would a wizard need a containment system?"

"I don't think it's for the wizard," I said.

"Then who's it for?" asked Shadow.

I looked at Dash. Dash looked at me. He let out a long sigh.

"Don't panic," he said, "but the wizard is dropping off a dragon."

"A dragon!" shrieked Whiskers.

Ding-dong!

This time we all jumped.

Ding-dong!

Dad ran up from the basement. He opened the door.

A very tall man stood dressed in full firefighting gear. He looked like he had just put out a fire.

CHAPTER
6

"Welcome, Fire Chief Morales," Dad
said.

"Sorry I'm late," said the fire chief. "We were
putting out a small brush fire."

"No problem," said Dad. "Thanks for coming on
a Saturday. Our special guest arrives tomorrow."

I shivered. The dragon was coming *tomorrow?*

"Let's make sure everything is as safe as possible," said the chief. "Can I see the room?"

Dad led the fire chief down to the basement.

Dash and I looked at each other with alarm. I could see he was shaking.

"What's everybody looking at?" asked Fuzzy and Furry. They poked their heads out of a heating vent in the Welcome Area. They looked a little dusty, but otherwise they were fine.

"What did you find out?" Dash asked.

"We had a few close calls," said Fuzzy.

"*Very* close," added Furry.

"Dad keeps coming downstairs," said Fuzzy.

"He's very nervous," added Furry.

"He almost stepped on us!" said Fuzzy.

"Twice!" added Furry.

"Guys," I said, "just tell us what you found out."

But before the gerbils could answer, I heard Jake shout from upstairs. "Where could they be? Start looking, Ethan!"

"Stop telling me what to do!" said Ethan.

"Start looking!" said Jake.

"You're not the boss of me!" shouted Ethan.

"Uh-oh," said Fuzzy. "I think we're in trouble."

"We'd better get back to the gerbiltorium," added Furry.

They disappeared into the heating vent. Dad and the fire chief came back upstairs.

"Thanks again," said Dad.

"Don't mention it," said Chief Morales.

"I was a little worried," said Dad.

"You did a great job. The new room is officially

up to safety code. But *please* be careful."

My ears perked up. Did he say "new room"? Did he say "be careful"?

Dad waved good-bye to Chief Morales. Then he headed straight back to the basement.

We all waited a moment. Then we quietly made our way toward the stairs. Dash stopped to collect some dog biscuits he had hidden under the sofa.

We went straight to Jake and Ethan's room. All except for Coco.

"Where are you going?" Dash asked her.

"My tummy tells me it's lunchtime," said Coco. "I'm going to find Cassie."

Fuzzy and Furry were already back, snug in their gerbiltorium.

"Report, please," Dash said.

"There's a new enclosure," Fuzzy said.

"It takes up one whole side of the basement," Furry added.

"It's big," Fuzzy said.

"Very sturdy," Furry added.

"It has sand and stones," Fuzzy said.

"Real stones," Furry added.

"There are two heat lamps," Fuzzy said.

"Very toasty," Furry added.

"There's a humidifier to keep the air moist," Fuzzy said.

"Like a jungle," Furry added.

"There's a new fire extinguisher," Fuzzy said.

"And a big first aid kit," added Furry.

"That's all we've got so far," Fuzzy said.

"But we are a little hungry," Furry added.

"Excellent job," I said.

Dash slipped the two dog biscuits through the bars of the gerbiltorium. "They're whole," he assured them. "No crumbs."

Fuzzy and Furry took a couple of bites.

Then they quickly buried the rest under the cedar shavings for later.

"Okay," said Dash. "What does this new information tell us?"

"The new guest needs a lot of space," I said.

"It likes heat and humidity," said Shadow.

"It needs to be separated from the other animals," Whiskers said, trembling, "which means it's *not* friendly."

"It might be friendly," said Dash.

"Then why do we need a first aid kit?" asked Whiskers.

"And a fire extinguisher?" asked Shadow.

"The dragon is going to burn down Animal Inn!" shrieked Whiskers.

"Let's stay calm," I said. "What if we give it a safe place outside where it can breathe its fire?"

"That sounds like a good plan," said Dash. "Like a campfire. Coco and I can collect wood on our afternoon walk."

"Wood for what?" asked Coco, coming in from lunch. She still had some mac-and-cheese on her nose.

"A special campfire," said Dash.

"Oh, goody," said Coco. "Will there be marshmallows?"

CHAPTER
7

Back in the Welcome Area, Cassie

put on Dash's leash.

Shadow rubbed against Cassie's leg.

Mom put on Coco's leash.

Shadow rubbed against Mom's leg. Shadow knows how to make a point.

"Okay, Shadow," Cassie said. "Mom, can Shadow come with us?"

Mom smiled. "Of course. Sometimes I think she's more dog than cat."

Cassie put on Shadow's leash. Yes, Shadow has a special cat leash.

Mom grabbed a big umbrella.

Ding-dong!

Mom opened the door. It was Martha, one of the Animal Inn groomers. While all of our groomers are excellent, Martha is my favorite. I just love the way she trims and files my toenails.

Yes, I have toenails. You might call them talons.

"Hi, Martha," Mom said. "Come on in. Cassie and I are taking the dogs out for a walk."

Shadow gave a loud meow.

"Correction," said Mom. "Cassie and I are taking the dogs and *Shadow* out for a walk. Then we'll check on the guests in the barn and kennels."

"Have fun," said Martha.

I watched as the group of walkers left through the front door.

"Hi, Leopold!" Martha waved. "How's my pretty bird?"

Did Martha know about the dangerous dragon? Would she have to groom its scales and trim its claws? A shiver ran down my back.

Ding-dong!

I froze in place. It's what we macaws do when we're scared.

Martha opened the door.

It was only Monsieur Petit, here for his weekly styling appointment. Monsieur Petit is a miniature French poodle. He is also one of my dearest friends. Monsieur has been coming to Animal Inn every Saturday since the day we opened.

"See you in an hour!" said Monsieur Petit's owner, Madame Gigi.

Then the phone rang.

"Be right back, Monsieur," Martha said, hurrying to the office.

"*Bonjour*, Leopold," Monsieur Petit crooned. "It's wonderful to see you."

I stayed frozen in place.

"What's the matter, *mon ami*?" Monsieur asked.

"We are expecting a new guest," I said. "A strange and scary guest."

"Scary?" Monsieur Petit asked. "Are you sure?"

"I'm not sure of anything," I said.

Monsieur Petit smiled. "This reminds me of a story," he said. "When I was a pup in Paris,

I heard some friends talking about a terrible
creature. They said it had horns and wings. I
was so scared. And then one day I looked up
and I saw the terrible creature perched high
above."

Monsieur Petit paused for a moment. I held my breath.

"It really was fierce and frightening," he said slowly.

"Oh dear," I gasped.

"But it was not dangerous." Monsieur Petit smiled. "It was a gargoyle. You do know, *mon ami*, what is a gargoyle?"

"Of course," I said. "It's a stone statue that guides rainwater away from a building."

"Correct," said Monsieur Petit. "I had nothing to fear. Perhaps you do not either."

"Ready, Monsieur?" Martha was back from the office. "Sorry to make you wait."

Monsieur Petit bowed to me, and then followed Martha to the grooming room.

I thought about what my wise friend had said.

Then I heard the sound of hammering. Dad was still working downstairs.

Unfortunately, he was not getting the basement ready for a gargoyle.

CHAPTER
8

"Looks like a storm is coming," said Jake as he came downstairs. The clouds were dark. The rain was now falling steadily.

Jake headed to the supply closet and grabbed the broom. Dragon or no dragon, there were still chores to be done.

"Want to help, Leopold?" Jake asked.

I flew over and took my place on Jake's shoulder.

Sweeping with Jake always calms me. He took me for a little ride around the Welcome Area. It felt safe.

Jake was careful not to get too close to Whiskers on the sofa. Brooms make Whiskers nervous. And Whiskers was nervous enough already.

"Come on, Jake," Ethan called from upstairs. "Time for chores."

"I know," Jake called back. "I'm sweeping the Welcome Area."

Ethan came down and slumped on the last stair. "I don't feel like doing chores today," he said.

"I know," said Jake, "but there are about a dozen guests on the third floor. I can't clean, feed, and water them all by myself."

"Why can't Cassie help?" asked Ethan.

"Cassie is helping Mom."

"Well, where's Dad?" Ethan said.

"Dad is busy finishing the new habitat," said Jake. "Aren't you excited about tomorrow? This is a big deal for Animal Inn."

"Yeah," said Ethan, "but new guests mean even more chores."

"Leopold is a pretty bird," I said. I wanted to cheer Ethan up.

I know what it feels like to be the middle child. Dash is older than me. Dash is the leader. Everybody looks up to Dash. Coco is younger than me. Coco gets to goof around, and everybody thinks she's adorable.

"Leopold is a pretty bird," I tried again.

"Hi, Leopold," Ethan said. He patted his knee. This was an invitation for me to go over.

"You want to come upstairs and help us with chores?" Ethan asked.

"Better late than never," I squawked.

"I guess that means yes," said Ethan.

We all headed up to the Reptile Room.

Chore number one—the Turtle Enclosure.

A box turtle named Bert was spending the week with us. His family was backpacking. No turtles allowed.

You might think that a box turtle would be staying in a box. But there you would be wrong. Box turtles are called "box turtles" because they can pull their heads, tails, and legs into their shells, and then close up like a . . . box. This is how they protect themselves in the wild.

Bert is lucky, I thought. *He has a built-in hiding place.*

Inside the turtle enclosure there was moss and ground-up tree bark. Ethan used a spray bottle to mist the moss with warm water, while Jake cleaned the pool. The pool was actually a paint tray filled with water. But it did the trick. Bert seemed quite pleased with his accommodations.

Then the boys rearranged the hideouts and climbing structures in the enclosure. Finally, Jake gave Bert a plate of worms, chopped spinach, and slightly mushy strawberries. Not my cup of tea, but Bert seemed to enjoy it.

Chore number two—the Snake Enclosure.

We moved on to Copernicus, the boa constrictor. He was curled up in his hiding box, taking an afternoon snooze. The snake enclosure was similar to the turtle's, just much bigger. Copernicus is almost five feet long.

Would he be in danger too when the dragon got here?

Outside, there was a rumble of thunder.

"Here comes the storm," said Jake.

Ethan checked the temperature and humidity in the enclosure. Jake made sure Copernicus had plenty of water. They didn't have to feed him, though. He had eaten just before he'd arrived. He wouldn't need another meal for a week.

Good thing too. A boa constrictor's favorite food is mice. And right next door, four generations of the Field family were enjoying a reunion.

Chore number three—the Rodent Room.

The Rodent Room is equipped with a system of tubes and tunnels. The pieces can be connected or disconnected, depending on how many different guests we have. There are wheels and swings and all kinds of toys. It can be a lively place.

Jake and Ethan filled the food bowls and water bottles.

What would a dragon do with a room full of mice? I shuddered at the thought.

Chore number four—the Small Mammal Room.

Our guests at the time included an Angora bunny named Juniper, a guinea pig named Squeaky, and a pair of ferrets named Frank and Bob. They each had their own hutch, except for the ferrets. They were bunking together.

Jake and Ethan scooped out the old cedar shavings. Then they sprinkled in new shavings. Once again they filled the food bowls and water bottles.

"Are we done yet?" asked Ethan. "This is taking forever."

I agreed. I needed to see if Dash was back.

"Almost done," said Jake. He swept up the

shavings that had fallen onto the floor. "You think this is tough. Just wait until tomorrow. That dragon is going to be a ton of work."

"Yeah," said Ethan. "But Dad will do most of it. He said we can't get too close because of the poison spit."

Poison spit? I gulped.

BOOM!

A clap of thunder shook the walls. Lightning flashed outside the windows. Rain poured down.

"Dragon spit is *not* poisonous," Jake said.

Thank goodness! I breathed a sigh of relief.

"It's *toxic.*"

CHAPTER
9

Toxic spit! Things were only
getting worse.

I flew downstairs to see if Dash, Coco, and
Shadow were back.

They barreled through the front door, startling
Whiskers, who was still on the sofa. Mom and
Cassie quickly undid the leashes and went upstairs
to change into dry clothes.

"So much for our plan," said Dash. "Not exactly campfire weather. Maybe the rain will dampen the dragon's fire."

I wanted to tell Dash that fire wasn't our only problem, but everyone looked frazzled. They didn't need to know about the toxic spit just yet.

"Did you gather any wood?" I asked. "In case the rain stops."

"No," Dash said. "There were ... complications."

"Coco got in trouble," said Shadow.

"I only wanted to play with the squirrel," said Coco. "I thought it was Curtis. Remember Curtis, who stayed with us that time? This squirrel looked just like Curtis."

"He looked *nothing* like Curtis," said Shadow. "Curtis was a red squirrel. The squirrel you were chasing was clearly a gray squirrel."

"I still think it was Curtis," Coco said.

BOOM!

Thunder stopped the argument.

BOOM! BOOM!

"We need a new plan," said Dash. "What are we going to do?"

"I know what *I'm* going to do," said Whiskers. "I'm going to hide under the sofa." Whiskers jumped down and crawled underneath.

"And I know what *I'm* going to do," said Shadow. "The next time that door opens, I'm out of here."

"And I know what *I'm* going to do," said Coco. "*I'm* going to be really friendly and helpful and give the dragon lots of mac-and-cheese. If it's full of mac-and-cheese, it won't have room to eat me. Or I might just hide under Cassie's bed."

"You'll never fit under Cassie's bed," scoffed Shadow.

"If anyone is going to hide under Cassie's bed, it's going to be me," Whiskers piped up. He crawled out from under the sofa. "I call Cassie's room! I think her door has a lock. Doesn't it?"

What was happening to us? It felt like we were falling apart, and the dragon wasn't even here yet.

Just then Fuzzy and Furry popped out of the heating vent.

"Dad's done downstairs," Fuzzy said.

"He's sweeping up," added Furry.

"It looks really cool," Fuzzy said.

"State of the art," added Furry.

"But what are we going to do?" Whiskers trembled.

I looked at Dash. Dash looked at me. We both thought for a moment.

"Perhaps we do nothing," I said. "We trust Mom and Dad's plan."

"Yes," said Dash. "They've never let us down before."

Shadow looked out at the pouring rain. Not the best weather for hitting the open road. "Okay," she said. "I'm in."

"Fine," said Whiskers. "But I still call Cassie's room."

CHAPTER
10

It was Dragon Day.

Mom quietly lifted the cover off my sleeping cage in Cassie's room.

"Good morning, Leopold," Mom whispered. Cassie was still asleep.

Between the raging storm outside and nightmares about dragons, I hadn't slept well.

I stretched my wings. Then I made my way

downstairs to the Welcome Area with Mom.

Animal Inn was very quiet. I looked out the window. Usually this was my favorite part of the day, at least when it was sunny. But today it was wet, windy, and gloomy.

A few minutes later Dash tiptoed down the stairs. He sat beside me and waited for Mom to go into the office.

"I couldn't sleep," I whispered.

"Me either," said Dash.

"I hope Mom and Dad know what they're doing," I said.

"Me too," said Dash.

Dad came downstairs next.

"Good morning, Dash. Good morning, Leopold," he said on his way to the office. "Today is the big day. Is everyone excited?"

Dash wagged his tail, but I could see his heart wasn't in it.

Whiskers came downstairs, pausing on each step. He looked around nervously. "Is it here yet?" he asked.

"Not yet," said Dash.

Whiskers scurried across the Welcome Area and hid under the sofa.

Jake and Ethan came downstairs next.

"Good morning, guys," said Ethan. "Did you hear that thunder last night?"

Jake looked out the window at the rain. "Things could get tricky today," he said. He leaned down to pat Dash's head. "But we'll figure it out, old buddy."

The boys went to the supply closet to get our breakfast ready. The lights flickered on and off.

"Uh-oh," said Jake. "I sure hope the power doesn't go out."

"That would be really bad," said Ethan.

Ethan brought my breakfast right to my perch. "Noble King Leopold," he said, and bowed. "Thy breakfast is served." I didn't feel like eating.

The boys went into the office to find Mom and Dad.

"If only King Leopold had a sword and armor," Shadow said, and then snickered, slinking down the stairs. "He could slay the—"

"Don't say that word!" Whiskers cried from under the sofa.

"What word?" said Coco, close behind Shadow. "You mean dra—"

BOOM!

A crack of lightning lit up the sky outside.

BOOM! BOOM!

"Aaahhh!" Whiskers screamed.

"It's just thunder and lightning," said Dash.

"I can't take one more thing!" whimpered Whiskers.

Ding-dong!

CHAPTER
11

Mom, Dad, Jake, and Ethan hurried

out of the office to answer the door.

Outside was a man dressed in a neon green rain suit. His jacket was crisscrossed with reflective stripes. He almost glowed.

Was this the wizard?

"Good morning," the man shouted over the sound of the rain. He pulled off the hood of his jacket. "I'm Mr. Washburn from the Reptile Rescue Center."

"Rescue?" I said to Dash. "Since when do dragons need rescuing?"

"We're the ones who need rescuing," Whiskers squeaked from under the sofa.

"Please, come in," said Dad.

From my perch I could see a truck in the driveway. There were two other figures dressed in the same neon green suits.

Three wizards?

The two figures were sliding a large, rectangular crate out of the back of the truck. There were lots of small holes along the sides of the crate. It looked like steam was rising off the top.

The two figures started for the front door. Lightning seemed to flash with every step they took.

"Guys," I whispered, "come look at this."

Dash and Coco put their paws on the windowsill. Shadow jumped up too.

"Is that it?" said Shadow. "I thought it would be bigger."

"Maybe it's a baby," said Coco. "I love babies."

"Pretty big baby," said Dash.

BOOM!

Thunder shook the window.

Jake came up behind us. "Hey, guys, I know you're curious to meet our new guest. But let's move away so the handlers can do their job."

I looked at Dash. *"Handlers?"* I said. "Not *wizards*?"

"I'm confused," said Coco.

"Join the club," said Shadow.

Dad held the door open while Mr. Washburn helped the two handlers bring in the crate.

"Where's Cassie?" Jake asked Ethan. "Doesn't she want to see this?"

"I don't know," said Ethan.

Steam was still rising off the crate. The handlers carried it across the Welcome Area, slowly and carefully. Mom opened the basement door.

We all huddled into a corner. Even Shadow was on guard.

"Easy does it," said Mr. Washburn as they made their way down the stairs. "Miss KD has had a long journey."

"Miss KD?" Coco said. "It's a *girl* dragon?"

CHAPTER
12

We heard a rattle in the heating

vent. Out popped Fuzzy and Furry. Even they looked shaky.

"We were just downstairs," said Fuzzy.

"With the green guys," added Furry.

"What did you find out?" I asked.

"They said it's not full grown," said Fuzzy.

"But it *is* a dragon," added Furry.

"It's the largest kind of dragon in the world," said Fuzzy.

"It's going to get really big," added Furry.

"It can run for short distances," said Fuzzy.

"A real sprinter," added Furry.

"And it eats almost any kind of meat," said Fuzzy.

"Including rodents," added Furry.

"*We're* rodents," said Fuzzy.

"So . . . we'll be in the gerbiltorium," added Furry. They quickly disappeared back into the heating vent.

Just then we heard the strangest noise coming from the basement. It was high-pitched and scary.

"Was that a *roar*?" I asked.

Mom, Dad, Jake, and Ethan were down there!

"We have to help them," said Dash. "First, we all run downstairs. Then Coco and I will growl the dragon into a corner."

"I can help too," said Shadow. She let out a very convincing hiss.

"I'll flap my wings and push the humans upstairs," I said.

"What can I do?" Whiskers asked. He crawled out from under the sofa.

"Very important," said Dash. "As soon as everyone is up here, you slam the door."

But before we could put our plan into action, Mom, Dad, Jake, Ethan, Mr. Washburn, and the two handlers all came up from the basement.

"Everything is great," said Mr. Washburn.

Great? I thought.

"Miss KD will be very happy here," said one of the handlers.

"Thanks," said Dad.

"We're excited to have her," said Mom.

"You have the care instructions," said Mr. Washburn. "Call us if you have any questions. We'll be back as soon as her new home is ready."

Mr. Washburn and the handlers said good-bye and headed for the truck.

"What's going on?" It was Cassie. She was wearing Mom's bathrobe. "Is it here?"

"Why are you wearing a bathrobe?" asked Ethan.

"It's not a bathrobe," said Cassie. "It's a *kimono*. To meet the kimono dragon."

Ethan rolled his eyes. "Cassie, it's a *Komodo* dragon, not a *kimono* dragon."

I looked at Dash. Dash looked at me. "A *Komodo* dragon?" I whispered.

"So where is it?" Cassie asked. "Where's the wizard?"

"Cassie, repeat after me," said Jake. "It's 'lizard,' not 'wizard.'"

Cassie tried hard to make the *L* sound, but it still came out sounding like "wizard."

"Wait," whispered Dash. "The wizard is a *lizard*?"

"I want to meet her!" said Cassie.

"Remember," said Dad, "you can visit Miss KD only with a grown-up."

"Let's have some breakfast first," said Mom, "and let Miss KD settle in."

Cassie frowned, but the Tylers headed upstairs.

The basement door was open just a crack.

"Follow me," whispered Shadow. "Let's investigate."

We crept down the stairs. Shadow first, then Dash and me, then Coco, and finally Whiskers.

"Where's the dragon?" asked Shadow.

"I think she's still in the crate," I said.

"Why?" asked Coco.

"Maybe it gives her a place to feel safe," said Whiskers.

Dash tiptoed over to the enclosure. He was cautious at first.

"Come here, guys," whispered Dash. "You'll never believe this."

The dragon was . . . *crying*.

That was the sound we had heard before. Our

fire-breathing, rodent-eating dragon was . . . *crying*?

"But why is she crying?" asked Coco. "I'm pretty sure dragons don't cry."

"Maybe she's scared," said Whiskers.

"Don't be scared," I said to our new guest. "We're excited to meet you."

We heard a few more sniffles. "Thank you," she said. "I'm Miss KD." To our surprise, her voice sounded small and frightened.

Suddenly a long yellow tongue appeared from the crate. It was forked at the end. It moved around, as if it were tasting the air.

Miss KD slowly crawled out. I could not connect the frightened voice to the body. Miss KD was as big as Dash. Maybe bigger.

She had a flat head, large claws, and a long tail.

In a word, she was magnificent.

CHAPTER
13

Fuzzy and Furry suddenly popped

out of a heating vent in the basement.

"Are you guys okay?" asked Fuzzy.

"We couldn't find you," added Furry.

"We're fine," I said. I pointed a wing toward the

enclosure. "Let me introduce Miss KD."

"Nice to meet you, my little mouse friends," said

Miss KD.

"Oh, we're not mice," said Fuzzy.

"We're gerbils!" added Furry.

Miss KD seemed a little embarrassed. "My apologies," she said. "I should be more careful, especially since folks are always confusing *me* for something *I'm* not."

"Like a dragon?" asked Shadow.

"Yes, sometimes," said Miss KD.

"Or a wizard?" asked Coco.

"Now, that's a new one." Miss KD smiled.

I cleared my throat. "Maybe I should explain," I said.

I told Miss KD everything that had happened since yesterday. And now it sounded so silly that we all started to laugh.

"It's an easy mistake to make," Miss KD said. "That's why we're called Komodo dragons. When humans first spotted us on the island of Komodo, they thought we *were* dragons. But we're really lizards. The people of Indonesia call us *ora*."

"What's an Indonesia?" Coco asked. "Is it something to eat?"

"Oh, no," Miss KD said, and chuckled. "Indonesia isn't a *what*. It's a *where*. It's a country in Southeast Asia. It's where I come from."

"Then how did you get here?" Shadow asked.

"That is a tale almost as long as my tail," Miss KD said. "But I'm happy to tell it."

We all settled in to hear her story.

"I started as an egg in a clutch on an island called Flores. Luckily, my mother was good at creating decoy nests. I hatched. Believe it or not, I was only thirty centimeters long when I was born."

Coco looked confused.

"About a foot," Dash explained.

"Exactly," Miss KD said. "I spent the first few years of my life high in the trees to avoid predators. When I turned four, I came down to the ground."

Miss KD paused for a moment, as if she were coming to the difficult part of her story.

"Then one day I came face-to-face with a human. He was shaking a big stick at me. I ran in the other direction, but I couldn't get away because he had helpers."

"What happened?" Dash asked.

"The next thing I remember," Miss KD said, "I was in a dark box that was too small for me. There was a loud noise all around, like the buzzing of hundreds of bees. I didn't know it at the time, but I was in an airplane. There were other creatures in cages too—a baby ape, four turtles, and a couple of snakes. We were scared and confused. We had been captured."

"That's terrible," Whiskers said.

"I wound up in Florida," Miss KD said. "It was hot and humid, just like home. But as I grew, my cage got too small. I wasn't getting the right kind of food. I started to get sick."

Miss KD paused and took a deep breath.

"I don't know how it happened, but one lucky day Mr. Washburn showed up with his truck and his friends. They took very good care of me. And now here I am with all of you."

"Welcome to Animal Inn," I said.

EPILOGUE

I learned a lot of important lessons

from Miss KD:

1. Sometimes scary things are not as scary as you think.

2. It's better to stick together than fall apart. (Especially when you're scared.)

3. Don't believe everything you've heard. (Especially if you've heard it from Cassie . . . or Coco . . . or Whiskers.)

4. Kimono is something to wear. Komodo
   is somewhere to visit.

One day Mr. Washburn returned to Animal Inn. The Reptile Rescue Center was ready for Miss KD. Like all other Animal Inn guests, Miss KD was moving on.

We promised to keep in touch. But that can be difficult when one of you is a scarlet macaw and the other one is a hundred-pound lizard.

I was settled on my perch in the Welcome Area the next day when Cassie came downstairs. She flopped onto the sofa. I could tell by her red, puffy eyes that she had been crying.

"Leopold, I'm so sad," she said. "I miss Miss KD."

I nodded.

"I know it's not fair to keep some animals as pets," she said, "but I really miss her."

I missed her too.

Then something near the window caught Cassie's attention.

"A butterfly!" she cried. "A real monarch butterfly!"

Cassie jumped up and ran to the door. "Here, little butterfly!" she called.

She ran outside, leaving the door wide open. It was an opportunity too good to miss. Shadow followed close behind. Even Whiskers peeked outside to see what all the excitement was about.

An ocean of orange-and-black wings flew overhead.

Mom ran outside, holding the reservations book.

"They're early," she said to herself. She was trying to hold the big book and turn pages at the same time. "I have them arriving next week."

"Beautiful butterflies!" Cassie called. "Welcome to Animal Inn!"

"Dad! Jake! Ethan!" Mom hollered. "All hands on deck. We have a lot of new guests to check in!"

FIND OUT WHAT HAPPENS IN THE NEXT **ANIMAL INN** STORY.

ANIMAL INN
Treasure Hunt

PAUL DUBOIS JACOBS & JENNIFER SWENDER

Welcome to Animal Inn. My name

is Dash. I'm a Tibetan terrier.

The day began like any other Saturday morning.

When I padded downstairs, the sun was just coming up. Mom was already in the Welcome

Area with a cup of coffee in one hand and a to-do list in the other.

Leopold was on his perch, his feathers neatly groomed. Leopold always likes to look his best.

"Good morning, Leopold," I said. "Nice day, isn't it?"

"Yes, Dash," Leopold agreed. "Nice and quiet."

Dad soon came downstairs with an armload of camping equipment.

"Did you find the poles?" Mom asked him.

Dad held up the tent poles. "Got 'em," he answered. "Are you sure you can manage here alone?"

"I'll be fine," Mom said, checking her to-do list. "It's going to be a quiet day."

I looked at Leopold. Leopold looked at me. Saturdays at Animal Inn are rarely quiet.

In fact, Saturday is our busiest day. Mom teaches her Polite Puppies class. Dad and Jake host the Furry Pages. That's when children read aloud to an animal buddy. Then there are grooming appointments and usually a birthday party or two.

"I've got it all worked out," Mom began. "Polite Puppies are going to join Furry Pages. That way I can run both programs at the same time. Plus, Mary Anne from the library is coming to give me a hand."

"Sounds like a great plan," said Dad.

My ears perked up. I love when Mary Anne comes to Furry Pages. She always brings cool books from the library.

"We only have one grooming appointment," Mom continued. "Monsieur Petit. Martha will do that. There are no parties, and we're not expect-ing any new guests."

"You're right," Dad said with a smile. "A quiet day."

I let out a sigh. We needed a quiet day.

The day before, we had said good-bye to 2,311 monarch butterflies. They had been spending a few days at our milkweed patch on their way to Mexico. During the previous few weeks waves of monarchs had been stopping at Animal Inn to relax and recharge.

Suddenly I heard Ethan from upstairs. "Where's *my* sleeping bag?" he hollered.

"I don't know," shouted Jake. "Did you put it in the pile?"

"Where's the pile?" Ethan asked.

"Yeah," chirped Cassie. "Where's the Nile? Is

that where we're camping tonight?"

"We're not camping on the Nile," said Ethan. "The Nile is in Africa."

"Ethan!" Jake shouted. "Did you feed Fuzzy and Furry?"

"I thought you fed them!" Ethan shouted back.

Mom looked at Dad. "Are you sure *you're* going to be okay?"

Dad smiled and shrugged. Then he hurried upstairs to help the kids.

A few minutes later Cassie and Coco came downstairs. Shadow followed in their . . . shadow. Shadow is supposed to be an indoor cat, but she loves to sneak outside.

"Don't tell anybody I'm here," Shadow whispered to Leopold and me. She snuck behind the sofa, ready to slip outside if given the chance.

"Princess Coco," Cassie said, pouting. "The campground says no dogs allowed. They're meanies."

"Good morning, Cassie," said Mom. "Are you excited to go camping?"

"Sort of," said Cassie. "I wish Coco could come. Maybe I can dress her up like a person." Cassie took off her jacket and tried to put it on Coco. Coco gave a big shake.

"Coco can help me with Polite Puppies and Furry Pages," Mom said. "Then she and I can take a nice, long afternoon nap." Coco flopped down on the floor with a sigh.

Dad, Jake, and Ethan came downstairs next. It was difficult to see them through the jumble of camping supplies they carried.

"Better late than never," Leopold squawked.

"Very funny, Leopold," said Ethan.

"Are you sure you'll be able to manage here alone?" Dad asked Mom again.

"Alone?" said Mom with a smile. "I've got Dash, Leopold, Coco, Shadow, and Whiskers."

"And Fuzzy and Furry," added Ethan.

"And don't forget the guests," said Jake. "You've got four frogs, a turtle, and two hamsters on the third floor, an alpaca in the barn, and a cat and three dogs in the kennel."

I had to agree. You're never really alone at Animal Inn.

SHARK SCHOOL

Dive into the world of Harry Hammer in this fin-tastic chapter book series!

Looking for another great book?
Find it
IN THE MIDDLE.

Fun, fantastic books for kids
in the in-be**TWEEN** age.

IntheMiddleBooks.com

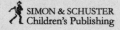